Dear Parent:

Congratulations! Your child is taking the first steps on an exciting journey. The destination? Independent reading!

STEP INTO READING® will help your child get there. The program offers books at five levels that accompany children from their first attempts at reading to reading success. Each step includes fun stories, fiction and nonfiction, and colorful art. There are also Step into Reading Sticker Books, Step into Reading Math Readers, and Step into Reading Phonics Readers— a complete literacy program with something to interest every child.

Learning to Read, Step by Step!

Ready to Read Preschool–Kindergarten
• big type and easy words • rhyme and rhythm • picture clues
For children who know the alphabet and are eager to begin reading.

Reading with Help Preschool–Grade 1
• basic vocabulary • short sentences • simple stories
For children who recognize familiar words and sound out new words with help.

Reading on Your Own Grades 1–3
• engaging characters • easy-to-follow plots • popular topics
For children who are ready to read on their own.

Reading Paragraphs Grades 2–3
• challenging vocabulary • short paragraphs • exciting stories
For newly independent readers who read simple sentences with confidence.

Ready for Chapters Grades 2–4
• chapters • longer paragraphs • full-color art
For children who want to take the plunge into chapter books but still like colorful pictures.

STEP INTO READING® is designed to give every child a successful reading experience. The grade levels are only guides. Children can progress through the steps at their own speed, developing confidence in their reading, no matter what their grade.

Remember, a lifetime love of reading starts with a single step!

www.stepintoreading.com

Educators and librarians, for a variety of teaching tools, visit us at
www.randomhouse.com/teachers

Library of Congress Cataloging-in-Publication Data
Scarry, Richard.
The best mistake ever! and other stories / Richard Scarry.
    p. cm. — (Step into reading. A step 3 book.)
SUMMARY: Three stories about Lowly Worm and his friends include "The Best Mistake Ever,"
"A Visit to Mr. Fixit," and "Best Friends."
ISBN 0-394-86816-1 (trade) — ISBN 0-394-96816-6 (lib. bdg.)
1. Children's stories, American. [1. Animals—Fiction. 2. Short stories.]
I. Title. II. Step into reading. Step 3 book.
PZ7.S327 Bb 2003 [E]—dc21 2002013233

Printed in the United States of America 52 51 50 49 48

STEP INTO READING

STEP 3

Richard Scarry
The Best Mistake
Ever!
And Other Stories

Random House 🏠 New York

The Best Mistake Ever

One day Mother Cat wanted
to clean the house.
Huckle Cat wanted to help.

He washed the dishes . . .

with too much soap.

He dusted the dust . . .

all over the room.

Huckle was no help at all.
"You can really help me
by going to the store,"
said his mother.
She made a shopping list.
"Here is what I need," she said.

"Butter,

cream,

apples,

potatoes,

and oranges."

Huckle wanted to help.
He ran to the store.

But he forgot to take
the shopping list!

His friend Lowly Worm
was at the store too.
"What is the matter, Huckle?"
asked Lowly.
"I am not sure
that I can remember
what Mother needs,"
said Huckle.
"Do not worry.
I will help you,"
said Lowly.

MILK

MEAT

"Butter? I think
Mother said 'butter,' "
said Huckle.

"I bet it was peanut butter,"
said Lowly.

He put a jar of peanut butter
in the shopping cart.

"Now let me see . . .
did she say 'cream'?"
said Huckle.

"Ice cream!

It must have been ice cream,"
said Lowly.

"Here is chocolate
and here is vanilla."

Huckle stopped
at a big box of apples.
"Apples?" he asked.

"Apple pie!
Apple pie with ice cream
is very good," said Lowly.

"Did she want potatoes?"

wondered Huckle.

"Better get potato chips.

Everyone likes potato chips,"

said Lowly.

And he pushed a big bag

into the cart.

"I think we have everything,"
said Huckle.

Just then Mr. Frumble
bumped into the oranges.

Oranges rolled everywhere.

"Thank you, Mr. Frumble!

I almost forgot the oranges,"
said Huckle.

But Lowly had a better idea.

"Get orange soda," he said.

"You need something to drink
with potato chips."

"Thanks, Lowly," said Huckle.

"We do need a good drink."

Huckle paid for the food.

"I will help you take it home,"
said Lowly.

Lowly opened the door

for Huckle.

"Hello, Mother," said Huckle.

"I got everything you wanted."

"Why, thank you, Huckle,"

his mother said.

Then she unpacked the bags.
"Huckle! This is party food!
I did not want these things!"

Just then the doorbell rang.

It was Aunty Rose

and her little girl, Lily.

"What a nice surprise!"

said Mother Cat.

Aunty Rose looked at the table.

"Oh," she said.

"Are you having a party?"

Mother Cat smiled.

"Why, yes," she said.

"Just for you!"

Everyone had a good time.

When the party was over,
Mother Cat said,
"Huckle, you really are
a big help.
Your shopping was
the best mistake ever!"

21

A Visit to Mr. Fixit

Huckle Cat was so happy.

He had just bought

the perfect Mother's Day present.

A cuckoo-cuckoo clock!

"Mother will love it,"
he said.

"Cuckoo!" went the clock.

It was one o'clock.

He put the clock
into the basket of his bike.
Then he set off for home
as fast as he could go.

"Not so fast!" said Lowly Worm.

"Slow down!"

But Huckle did not slow down.

He turned the corner and
CRASHED
right into Postman Pig.
"Cucko-o-o-o-o!" went the clock.

Officer Murphy came right over.

"Oh, no! The clock is broken!"
said Huckle.

"You are lucky
that is all that is broken,"
said the police officer.

"You were going too fast.
And you did not ring
your bell."

Huckle said, "I'm sorry,
but my bell is broken."

Officer Murphy told Huckle
to get his bell fixed.

Huckle and Lowly went
to Mr. Fixit's store.
"Can you fix my bike bell
and this cuckoo-cuckoo clock?"
asked Huckle.
"Of course I can,"
said Mr. Fixit.
"Come back in an hour
and your bell and clock
will be as good as new."

Huckle and Lowly left the store.

Mr. Fixit set to work.

He took the bell apart.

He took the clock apart.

"Now, let me see . . ." he said.

When Huckle and Lowly came back,
Mr. Fixit had everything
back together again.
"Oh, thank you, Mr. Fixit!"
said Huckle.
"Glad to be of help,"
said Mr. Fixit.

Huckle could hardly wait
to give his mother the clock.
He got to his house
and rang his bike bell.
"Cuckoo-cuckoo!" went the bell.
Huckle was very surprised.

Cuckoo-cuckoo!

Then he gave the clock

to his mother.

"Happy Mother's Day," he said.

"Dring-dring!" went the clock.

Huckle was very surprised.

So was his mother.

"What a wonderful clock!"

she said.

"I have never seen

a cuckoo-cuckoo clock

that sounds like a bike bell!

Thank you so much, Huckle!"

Huckle loved

his new bike bell, too.

There was not another one

like it in Busytown!

He rushed off to thank

Mr. Fixit for the mixup.

And when he turned the corner,

he rang his bell.

"Cuckoo-cuckoo!"

Best Friends

Huckle Cat and Lowly Worm
were best friends.
They did everything together.
They walked to school together.

They sat together.

They always played
together at playtime.

At snack time every day
Huckle and Lowly got
the milk and cookies
for the class.
Miss Honey was happy
to have such good friends
in her class.

And after school
they played together
at Huckle's house.

But one morning
Huckle waited and waited
for Lowly.
"Hurry, Huckle,
or you will be late
for school,"
said Officer Murphy.

Huckle ran to school.
He hoped that
Lowly was not sick.
Today was Huckle's birthday.
He wanted to show
his birthday presents
to Lowly after school.

Huckle ran into his classroom.

He was surprised

to see Lowly.

He was even more surprised

to see Lowly sitting

with Willy Rabbit.

"What is the matter?

Are you mad at me?"

asked Huckle.

But Lowly did not answer.

He just giggled.

Then Lowly whispered

something to Willy

and they both giggled.

Suddenly Huckle felt sad.

At playtime Lowly was busy
whispering to everyone—
everyone but Huckle.
Huckle felt even sadder.

At snack time Miss Honey said,
"Today Lowly and Willy
will get our snack."
Huckle felt awful.
"This is the worst day
of my life!" he thought.

Soon Lowly and Willy
came back.
"Surprise!" said Lowly.
They were carrying
a birthday cake!

The whole class sang
"Happy Birthday" to Huckle.
Then Huckle made a wish
and blew out the candles.

"What was your wish?"
asked Lowly.
"I cannot tell you or
it will not come true,"
said Huckle.

Then Miss Honey cut the cake
and everyone had a piece.
"Hmmm, good!" said Huckle.

After school Huckle and Lowly
played with Huckle's
new train set.

"This morning I was afraid
that you did not want to be
my best friend anymore,"
said Huckle.
"I will always be
your best friend,"
said Lowly.

Huckle was very happy.

His birthday wish

had come true.

He and Lowly would always be

best friends.